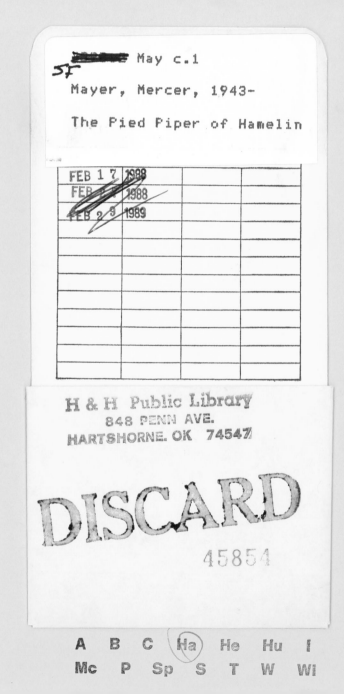

THE PIED PIPER OF HAMELIN

THE PIED PIPER OF HAMELIN

AS TOLD AND ILLUSTRATED BY

◇ MERCER MAYER ◇

Macmillan Publishing Company   New York   ◇   Collier Macmillan Publishers   London

Macmillan Publishing Company

866 Third Avenue, New York, NY 10022

Collier Macmillan Canada, Inc.

Printed and bound in Japan

First American Edition

10 9 8 7 6 5 4 3 2 1

The text of this book is set in 14 point Goudy Old Style.
The illustrations are rendered in pen-and-ink and watercolor
on Strathmore watercolor paper.

Library of Congress Cataloging-in-Publication Data

Mayer, Mercer, date.

The Pied Piper of Hamelin.

Summary: The Pied Piper pipes the village free of
rats, and when the villagers refuse to pay him for the
service he pipes away their children as well.

1. Pied Piper of Hamelin (Legendary character)

[1. Pied Piper of Hamelin (Legendary character)

2. Folklore—Germany (West)—Hamelin] I. Browning,
Robert, 1812-1889. Pied Piper of Hamelin. II. Title.

PZ8.1.M462Pi 1987 398.2'1'0943 87-1607 ISBN 0-02-765361-7

For

◇ Judith Whipple ◇

friend and editor

who understands the creative process

Many years ago a stranger walked upon an open road. He had walked for miles, and the dust of the road covered his cloak and stung his eyes. There was a look about him so mysterious and strange that all who passed by stayed far to the other side. The road he traveled wound over a hill. Below ran the river Weser, and beyond rose the walls of the town of Hamelin. The stranger stopped to rest, for he had traveled long and now his journey's end was in sight. As he rested, he gazed at the town below.

Hamelin was a beautiful town of whitewashed houses and neatly kept streets. One would have thought that those who lived there were happy and content, and that would have been true, except for the rats.

Rats! Where they came from, no one knew, but come they did by the thousands. They filled the streets. They hid in walls. As bold as brass they chattered back at anyone who defied them. They bullied the dogs and killed the cats.

Nursery maids were hard-pressed to keep the children safe. The rats burrowed through floors, scratched through walls, and gnawed past chains and locks. Anything left for just a minute the rats would claim for a nest—men's hats, cheese vats, balls of yarn, babies' cradles—anything!

Women with long hair were often surprised to find a rat living in their curls. No one could have a quiet conversation, for the rats would chime in, mimic and tease and mock. No one could eat without sharing a bite, or perhaps a whole dinner, with a sudden horde of hungry rats.

No larder could be sealed against them. They filled up chimneys with their nests and pushed the swallows from their eaves. The chickens would not lay eggs, and the cows were too nervous to give milk. The dry-goods stores were left in shambles. Fine bolts of cloth at the tailors' were soiled by their wet little feet.

No place was considered sacred by these vermin. Not even the great cathedral was spared. No minister or priestly man could conduct a holy service without the accompaniment of shrieking, chattering, and squeaking.

Their leader, it was said, was a great ugly gray rat twice the size of the others. He planned and schemed, for it was his dream to drive away the people and have a rat town of his very own. He was said to be as clever as any devilish creature born under the sun. It was even said that he spoke five languages, but this was purely gossip, for we all know that rats can't talk.

Leading the citizens of Hamelin in their fight against the rats were the able-bodied council of the town and its magnificent leader, the mayor. If by magnificent is meant fat, he was most certainly that. He and the council members talked of nothing but rats, usually over great lunches of roast beef, stuffed goose, fine wines, and all the other tidbits that help highly placed, important people do their jobs. They ate and drank their way through many taxpayer dollars in their eager pursuit of the solution to the rat problem. Much food and many words passed back and forth along the table; but as for solutions, none were found.

On one particular day, the townsfolk decided to address the problem directly. They called a town meeting, then went to the town hall to inform the council of the citizenry's demands. In a great body they stormed into the meeting chamber, where lunch had just finished. Their leader, the fishmonger's wife, cried, "Get rid of the rats promptly or we shall take pleasure in coating your ample bodies with tar sprinkled with chicken feathers, and thereafter throwing the lot of you into the river." In those days town meetings could be very heated affairs.

"How marvelous," said the mayor, being a politician to the core, "that all of you concerned citizens should come to see us directly. That's community spirit, for you. As for the rats, we have just come to a solution, which we are sure shall work. Do not fear. We shall most certainly clean them out of town, posthaste."

The great body of concerned citizens left—if not quietly, at least quickly.

The mayor mopped his brow and composed himself. "It's time," he said, "if we value these delicious lunches and our jobs, and perhaps our very lives, it's time to do something about the rats. But, oh, how I loathe the very thought of them."

Suddenly the town hall shook from its very foundations. "What was that?" said the mayor.

The council members stood silent. The air grew dark, as though a hand had passed before the sun. The building trembled and heaved again, and the windows rattled and gave off a whistling sound. "It is a strange wind blowing through town," said one.

With that came a loud knocking at the door. Each looked to the other, but no one spoke. The mayor finally called out, "Come in!" and puffed himself up to show his authority.

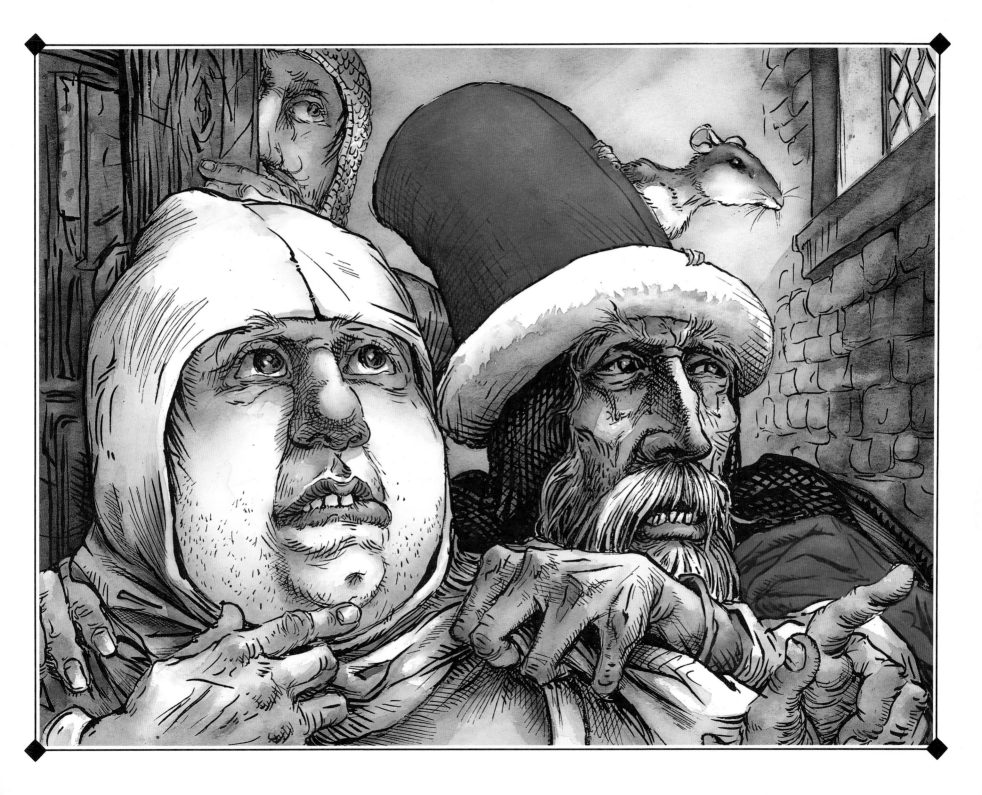

The door swung open and in came a man, very tall and thin, with blond hair and tanned skin. From his shoulders hung a strange cloak as long as he was tall, all checked in red and yellow. A wide-brimmed hat shaded his eyes. Like two pins the eyes were, and blue.

He stood before the council table. "Excuse me, sirs," said he. "I see that your lovely town is plagued with vermin. For that very reason I have come to talk to you. You see, I have a way to draw after me all creatures that live beneath the sun. None can resist my spell."

The council members cast sidelong glances at one another and scoffed.

"You might wonder," continued the stranger, "what qualifications I have for such a job as this. But, here, let me show you." He paused, slowly waved his arm in the air, and the room darkened even more. Then he spoke, and his words became pictures that filled the room with a life of their own.

"I saved the Sultan of Swazoo and his kingdom from a plague of scorpions. In India I banished vampire bats. There were toads in Ethiope. One dragon and reptiles great and small I have caused to flee. Ah, yes, and spiders—spiders are my specialty. So rats are nothing, take my word, for it's as good as my name. I am called the Pied Piper."

The mayor, observing the strange visions filling the room, broke into a cold sweat, jumped to his feet, and said, "We take your word. We do, we do! Now put this room in order before I faint."

With a wave of his hand the piper wiped away the images.

"We'll pay whatever you wish to rid us of these rats. One thousand. No, ten. No, fifty thousand in royal silver."

"One thousand will do fine," said the piper, with a twinkle in his eye. Stepping from the hall, he raised his pipe to his lips and blew a note so sweet that it made one believe that all creatures in heaven and on earth were finally well and at peace. As he walked he played on, and all that heard him were transfixed. The music filtered deep down within Hamelin town, to touch each and every rat. So compelling was the sound that the rats rushed out in droves to seek the source of the wondrous music.

They leaped through windows, poured forth from doors, scampered from cupboards. Soon the streets of Hamelin were a teeming flood of rats, all following the Pied Piper. There were fat rats, skinny rats, black rats, brown rats, gray rats, old rats, young rats. Whole families followed him—cousins, uncles, brothers, and sisters—dancing and prancing, pushing and shoving, all wishing to be first in line.

He walked through the south gate of the city and stood by the river's edge. Before the astonished eyes of the watching townspeople, every last rat plunged joyously into the river and drowned.

All but one. That rat found his way back to the rat kingdom. This was his report.

"As the piper began to play, it was as if the world was made for rats alone. To be near him was to be full and content. To listen to the music was like being in the fattest larder that ever was."

Needless to say, the king of the rats found the survivor quite daffy and sent him to the doctors, to let them try and unravel his mixed-up ratty wits.

As the Pied Piper walked back through the streets of town, the people cheered and patted him on the back. The mayor ordered all the bells to be rung. "Plug up the rats' holes. Rip out their nests," he commanded.

The Pied Piper walked up to the mayor and stretched out his hand. "One thousand pieces of the king's silver, if you please," he said.

The mayor began to choke, for with that the town council could eat pheasant every day for a month. "Surely you jest, to pay such a sum to a fellow who simply wanders by. But, of course, let no man deny that you've done the job well. But, after all, it's not as though you toiled and sweated for weeks. Here, let me give you twenty-five. That's more than most make in a month."

The piper's face grew grim and tense. "I do not bargain with sultans, kings, or the likes of you. Settle your debt with me as agreed, or you might find me piping in a way you do not like."

"Don't threaten me, you vagabond," said the mayor. "I could have you flogged and stuffed into prison for such insolence. But, here, let's not quibble. Take fifty for your work—it's better than nothing at all."

The piper did not reply. He smiled a strange, thin-lipped smile and bowed. Then he turned to the crowd. "Does no one here find my fee just?"

The crowd murmured among themselves, and then someone shouted, "One thousand pieces of the king's silver to play a silly tune. Go on!" With that the crowd began to boo and hiss. This made the mayor puff up even more.

A small child pulled at the piper's cape. "Thank you," he said, "for ridding our town of the rats."

The piper smiled broadly and touched the eager youngster on the head.

He turned again to the mayor. "At first I thought I might deliver to this town more trouble than it has ever seen, but that would be unfair to the innocents who live here. I have decided instead to spare them from the likes of you."

The mayor and all those within earshot looked baffled.

The Pied Piper turned around and walked away, and as he walked he played his pipe. From every household came, running and laughing, the children of Hamelin. Bringing up the rear was a little lame boy who struggled with all his might to keep up. They followed the piper down the streets of town, then crossed the bridge, and were gone. The townspeople, who tried to follow, found themselves unable to move, as if their feet were nailed to the ground.

When at last the music faded away, there was not a trace of the piper or the children. Then one small boy came running, with wonder in his eyes. "It's the lame boy," someone said. "But he's no longer lame!"

The little boy spoke to them, and as he did it seemed that the magic of the piper was upon him, for the words he spoke became a picture that everyone could see. "We reached a door in the mountainside, and all the children went through. As I was about to enter, the piper touched my shoulder. He said that if I returned to tell what happened, I would be healed and later he would come for me if I wished. Though I shall miss my friends, I am here to tell you they are safe and happier than ever."

Here is the story that was told by the little lame boy who was healed by the piper. The boy grew up to be a bard. On the roads and in the towns he sang this song:

I remember when the piper came piping
the promises given, the pledges that were made.
There will be weeping, there are no children sleeping,
they have all gone away, for the piper must be paid.

Late at night when the sky is clear and frosty,
a melody still lingers, deep in heaven's blue.
A haunting reminder, they could have been kinder.
The piper knocking at your door will take what is due.

Now like paupers they look upon the mountain
that towers above them, their children fast within.
But mountains can't be opened by words or by tokens;
a promise is a promise and this story now must end.